First published in Great Britain in 1993
by Heinemann Young Books Limited.
This edition published 1999 by Mammoth,
an imprint of Egmont Children's Books Limited
239 Kensington High Street, London, W8 6SA

ISBN 0 7497 3500 7

10 9 8 7 6 5 4 3 2 1

A CIP catalogue record for this book
is available from the British Library

Printed in Great Britain by Cox & Wyman Ltd,
Reading, Berkshire

Contents

If you enjoy reading this book, you might
also like to try another story
from the MAMMOTH STORYBOOK series:

chapter 1

Valley Road Primary had seen better days. It huddled under the high wall of the chemical works. It had tall black ventilators like witches' hats, soot-spotted brickwork, railings round the yard with spikes, and its windows were too high up for the kids to see out of. You had to go to the toilet through the pouring rain, and when you got there, all the locks had been kicked off the cubicle doors.

When the chemical works had been working, no kid had ever had colds or flu. The chemical workers next door didn't either. They said no germs could live in the sulphur-laden atmosphere. But now the chemical works was dead, just so much rusty

steel hanging up in the sky, with loose sheets of corrugated iron that banged loudly every time the wind blew.

The kids were always bored and weary. Weary from staying up too late to watch telly. Bored because lessons about all the sheep in Australia or ways to make our country green again seemed total Dragsville after last night's video of *Dirty Harry*. The teachers despaired of teaching them anything, but went on talking and talking because that was their job and they had to earn their money. The teachers counted the minutes till the bell went when they could dive into the staffroom for a quick cup of coffee or jump into their middle-aged cars and drive off to where the fields were green and the air didn't smell of rotting soot.

The Head sat in her office. Once she had dreamed of happy rosy faces, eagerly waiting to be taught about life. Now she just filled in forms for the county council and lectured the naughtiest children over and over again, knowing that if she talked till she was blue in the face they still wouldn't listen to a word she said.

She used to think she ran the school. Now she had a sinking feeling that the school was run by the two worst boys in the fourth year, Taffy Thomas and Edward Druel. Taffy was the second-worst boy in the school and Edward was the worst: Mafia godfathers in anoraks.

It was on one of the brighter mornings, when the weak white sun was struggling through the smog of the valley, that the black cat came walking in the yard gate. Or at least between the gateposts, for the gates had collapsed under much swinging by the kids. Now there were just iron hooks sticking out, upon which victims were hung by the collars or belts and left choking and yelling.

The cat crossed the yard.

The school doors were open; the cat slipped through. It prowled up the corridor, listening to the grumbling snarling rumble that came from the classrooms; from kids who'd lost their books, not done their homework, whose pens had run out or who were being jabbed in the back with biros. Any excuse not to work . . .

The cat chose the slightly-open door of the classroom from which the second-worst noise came, and slipped in. Few cats would have dared. Most cats would have known instinctively they would be kicked, have their tails trampled on, be yelled at or grabbed and half-strangled. But this cat trotted swiftly across the room before anyone noticed it; and for some reason known only to itself, jumped up on the desk of Taffy Thomas, sat down, and looked him straight in the eye.

An awed silence fell. Few were the boys who dared look Taffy straight in the eye, let alone a cat. Taffy was a sight to frighten the eye of any beholder, a medium-sized barrel of muscle. His eyes, always reduced to slits, made him look like Genghis Khan with blond hair the length and texture of a worn scrubbing-brush. His fists were usually clenched for a blow, and kids swore his boots had bloodstains on the toecaps.

But the very nerve of the cat made Taffy pause. That and the flattering fact that the

6

cat had picked *him* out. The cat was large, though very thin. Its ears were notched with the scars of many battles, which was the thing that first impressed Taffy. Its fur lay in the most interesting whirls on its face and round its nose. Taffy had never seen a cat close-to before. To him, cats were stinking slinking things, that kept a wary eye open for boys throwing bricks, and the leather-jacketed men who walked their Dobes and German Shepherds round his council estate.

He had an impulse to reach out and stroke the interesting whirls of fur, the battered ears . . .

The cat rubbed its head against his hand and began a ragged purring. It was the first creature in a long time that had shown pleasure in Taffy's attentions. And even the worst tyrant has a need to feel loved by *something*.

'Ey, cat,' said Taffy, 'you're all right.'

With those words, the cat achieved instant safety in Valley Road Primary. He became one of Taffy's people. Like Swotty Knowles, who hung around Taffy's elbow and was his wise man; who told Taffy every fact about Patagonia or nuclear fission or fractions that he needed to know. Like Leggy Hayes, who ran Taffy's errands for him, faster than any other boy in the school could run. Like Lee Ho, whose father ran the local takeaway and was always good for a bag of free chips for every member of Taffy's gang. Like Fingers Newcome, who did Taffy's shoplifting for him. And Gazzer Brown and Roly Powley, who would have cheerfully given their lives for Taffy in battle. Taffy was a beast, but a just beast. You looked after him, he looked after you.

All the kids in the class clustered round.

'Can I stroke your cat, Taffy?' asked Lorraine Everett.

With a nod, Taffy indicated that she could. They all pushed and jostled to stroke it, careful not to jostle Taffy. He sat back with a satisfied smirk.

At her desk, Miss Morgan watched warily and took a breather. It was nice to have ten minutes when utter chaos did not threaten.

Finally, when everybody had stroked the cat, Taffy looked at the forest of waving, stroking hands and said, 'Enough'.

10

And every hand instantly vanished. Taffy looked at Miss Morgan and said, 'Can the cat stay, miss?'

Miss Morgan took a deep breath. Cats in classrooms were probably against county regulations; but it was so nice to see the children really interested in *something*; enough to stop the non-stop bickering, the concealed kicking under the desks and the half-concealed punching above them.

'Yes,' she said. 'If you're *good*.'

Taffy gave the class a look. The class sank back into their seats and a deathly hush fell. They even looked at Miss Morgan, as if expecting to be taught something.

Miss Morgan had long since given up hope of interesting them in anything. She'd tried to tell them about her trip to Florida, but they just yelled, '*Miami Vice!*' She'd tried telling them about her previous holiday in Jersey, but they all just groaned, '*Bergerac!*'

She thought sadly that even if she sailed up the Orinoco, or climbed Mount Everest or voyaged to Mars, some wretched character on TV would have got there before her.

But she loved cats. They had four at home on the farm in North Wales, who got up to all kinds of tricks.

Now she told Taffy things he wished to know; tales of giant rats killed in heroic battles; of eggs stolen from the henhouse by the most cunning possible means; of kittens carried home by their mothers through blizzards; of a cat that found its way back home after having been given away to a lady in Aberystwyth, a hundred miles away. She satisfied Taffy better than Swotty Knowles did. He sat, nodding at her every word, like a Mafia godfather receiving the report of a lieutenant who has done extremely well. And the rest of the class, at first silent only through fear of Taffy, became enthralled for their own sakes.

And the cat sat on Taffy's desk, purring, never taking its eyes off Miss Morgan's face. As if she was telling the whole history of its great nation, and telling it with great accuracy.

chapter 2

Mrs Forbes, the Head, on her way to quell excessive rioting in another class, glanced through the glass of their classroom door and saw a sight that truly amazed her.

A teacher teaching, to a total silence; a class in which every child was absorbed, taking in every word.

Then she saw the black cat, sitting on the desk. Which was, of course, against county regulations . . .

She slipped into the classroom. Not a child even looked round. She too became enthralled by Miss Morgan's eloquence about cats.

Finally, the bell went, and the children

saw and noticed her for the first time. And all the girls, who as usual sat next to the door, rushed to tell her about the cat and cats in general.

That was how things had been, when Mrs Forbes started teaching thirty years ago, in a little school in the heart of the country. Children who rushed to tell you things, children who couldn't wait to share, children whose tongues were tripping over each other with enthusiasm. It seemed a more incredible miracle than the loaves and fishes.

And then came Taffy Thomas's stentorian question, flung right across the classroom.

'Can the cat stay, miss?'

'But it must belong to someone,' she stammered.

'No, miss, it's a stray, miss. It's terribly thin. All its ribs are sticking out. And it hasn't got no collar.'

Mrs Forbes was a realist. It was against

the rules, yes. But what county official had ever dared stick his head through the doors of Valley Road? Who would know? And, if it had this effect . . .

'But who will take responsibility for feeding it?'

Taffy looked at Lee Ho. Lee Ho said, his face suitably inscrutable, 'I will bring fresh chicken-skin. I will bring fresh fish-skin. The cat will not starve.'

'And we'll bring milk, miss,' chorused the girls, led by Lorraine.

'But what if it gets ill? Who'll pay for the vet?'

'We'll start a fund, miss,' said Taffy, and he nodded to Gazzer Brown, who ran the protection-racket for him, and relieved certain kids of their dinner-money.

Mrs Forbes shuddered inwardly. But then Lorraine and Tracy and Diane were getting money out of their purses, and thrusting it at her.

And so the cat fund began.

'Yes,' said Mrs Forbes. 'He can stay. If you're good.'

After break, it was maths. And maths was the lesson Miss Morgan dreaded above all others; the one when the worst riots broke out.

Even on this miraculous morning they became noisy and quarrelsome. The brief miracle seemed to be over.

But as the noise increased, the cat grew restless. Began to swish his tail, and look longingly towards the door.

'He don't like this noise,' shouted Taffy. 'Shurrup!'

There was a shocked silence. Did it mean they had to behave, even in *maths*?

In the silence, the cat relaxed again, and began to wash himself.

They took the point. They had to behave, even in maths.

Miss Morgan, searching her mind desperately for something exciting on the dull topic of percentages, found herself inspired. The vast amount of income tax that the government was stealing from their dads; the VAT on a Mars Bar, or a packet of onion-flavoured Twizzles . . .

Somehow, together, they got through it in peace.

Chapter 3

By the end of lunch-time, the whole school knew about the cat. The cat stayed close to Taffy; Taffy's gang closed round it protectively. But people from other classes were allowed to stroke it, one by one, except Edward Druel. It kept its cool and charm, even though it must have felt its skin and fur were being worn away by all the stroking hands. There were humble offerings of cheese-and-onion crisps, which the cat ate delicately, cocking its head on one side, then finishing up the crumbs and smelling the concrete of the yard to make sure there was nothing left. Sweets were forbidden, as being bad for the cat's teeth. At the end of the

lunch-hour, back in the classroom, Lee Ho opened his first delicious-smelling packet of steaming chicken-skin, and the whole class waited with bated breath, and heaved a deep sigh of satisfaction when the cat ate the last scrap. They felt its belly, and exclaimed how it bulged, afterwards.

By afternoon break, requests were coming in from the other teachers, for the cat to visit their classrooms. Miss Morgan, in consultation with Taffy, declared the cat would make a tour of the school at half past three.

'If they're *good*,' added Taffy.

Such a hush fell in the classrooms as Mrs Forbes had never heard in all her time at Valley Road.

The teachers seized their chance, and taught like men and women inspired. Essays were set and worked on with great fervour. 'The Sort of Cat I Would Like to Have', 'Pets We Have Kept', 'Chased by a Tiger in the Indian Jungle' and even 'Batman versus Cat-woman'.

Taffy returned from his Royal Tour, beaming all over his face. 'They all behaved smashing,' he announced. 'Except Batty Williams. He trod on the cat's tail. I'll have to thump him after school.'

Miss Morgan pleaded with him earnestly to give Batty Williams a second chance. In the end, Taffy nodded graciously. Batty Williams would be reprieved this time. Taffy was enjoying being a public benefactor; and some dim sense warned him that public benefactors did not thump people.

There were great arguments at home time about where the cat should sleep. But by the time they had finished arguing, and had decided the caretaker's hut was warmest, and nobody cared if it got piddled in, they realised the cat itself had solved the problem. By vanishing.

But he was there again in the morning, bright and early, for his packet of steaming fish-skin.

chapter 4

By the third day, even the weariest and most disillusioned parents had heard. Fresh-faced excited kids are hard to resist, even when you're sitting clapped-out in your chair with your first can of lager of the evening, and your head is about to burst after eight hours' din in the canning-factory or digging up the road with a pneumatic drill. Parents spoke kindly of Valley Road for the first time in years, instead of calling it 'that awful dump'. Little gifts of food and money began to arrive for the cat. Certainly more than enough money to buy him a very grand collar and a medallion with his name on.

'What do you call him?' asked Mrs Forbes.

'Just The Cat,' said Taffy, who was not a poetic soul.

'He's got very big feet,' said Swotty Knowles. 'If he wore boots he would take size twelve. Let's call him Bigfoot, after that monster –'

Taffy's elbow shot out like lightning and Swotty doubled up with a groan. Any insult to the cat was an insult to Taffy. Mrs Forbes let her gaze slide away out of the window;

as a fellow-leader, she did understand the need for group-discipline, even there in her own study.

But the name stuck. Not Bigfoot, but Size Twelve.

Size Twelve went on to the medallion. Size Twelve was given his collar in assembly in front of the whole school, to much applause, while Taffy held him.

Afterwards it was generally agreed that he enjoyed wearing the collar; he scratched his neck twice as often, just for the pleasure of making his bell tinkle.

It was a week before the local press got on to the story of the cat that came to school for lessons. A reporter-photographer turned up. Mrs Forbes was appalled.

But then the reporter had the sense to remark how well-behaved the school seemed. So different from the reports he'd heard . . .

Mrs Forbes took a deep breath, and burnt her boats. The reporter was, after all, a parent . . . She sat and talked to him and poured her heart out. After all, the reporter was just from the local free paper; none of the high-ups at County Hall would possibly read anything as despised as the local freeby . . .

It was a very a nice photograph, with Taffy in his best jumper looking positively benevolent. More like the Chinese god of good luck than Genghis Khan. And the article said how school life was bucking up because of Size Twelve, in spite of all the leaking roofs, and the paint hanging off the walls in great flapping flakes, and a shortage even of drawing-pins . . .

Chapter 5

The fourth-year parents' night fell a week later. Normally about seven depressed parents turned up. That night there were over sixty. Mrs Forbes could have sworn that they'd only come to see the famous cat. What a pity that Size Twelve could not have been there to greet them! But he always vanished at home-time.

And then, just as she was about to open the meeting, Taffy walked in with Size Twelve in his arms, to enormous applause. They had spent, he said, the intervening hours hidden away in the games cupboard. He had known all the parents would want to see Size Twelve.

Size Twelve sat demurely on the Head's table throughout the meeting. His yellow eyes flicked across with interest to watch anyone who raised their hand to ask a question. When it was a hostile question (and there were a few) his tail lashed angrily. When someone else said something helpful, he purred loudly. It was almost as if, Mrs Forbes thought a trifle wildly, he not only understood everything that was said, but was actually *running* the meeting.

Taffy sat on the edge of the dais below, swinging his legs and quite at ease. But his eyes never left the cat; there was a look of dumb adoration in them that made Mrs Forbes wonder which one of them was the king, and which the subject. Did Taffy own Size Twelve, or did Size Twelve own Taffy? Stop it, she told herself; you're going soft in the head in your old age . . .

But she had little enough time to wonder.

It wasn't the usual dull meeting. The parents might have come in the first place to see Size Twelve; but they'd read how the school was struggling, and they suddenly got angry about the way their children's education was suffering. They wanted to help, raise funds. What did the school need? A computer, a mini-bus? Mrs Forbes was on the verge of tears.

'Paint, mainly,' she said through gritted teeth. 'A fresh coat of paint to brighten up the children's lives.'

One parent jumped up and said, 'I'm in the painting trade, missus!'

Mrs Forbes took one look at his muscle-barrelled body and amiable Genghis Khan expression and said faintly, 'Mr Thomas?'

'The same. You've made a real difference to my lad. He can't wait to get to school in the mornings, now. He's gone by eight, and his mother doesn't even have to call him. He

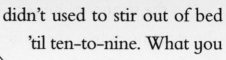

didn't used to stir out of bed 'til ten-to-nine. What you want painting? I could do a nice job on this hall, and it won't cost you a penny beyond the price of the paint.'

It all led to the start of a parents' committee, the first Valley Road had ever had. Mr Thomas was voted chairman.

'There's a little spare money in the Size Twelve Fund,' said Mrs Forbes timidly.

That was the first the parents had heard of the Size Twelve Fund. By the time they left that night, the Size Twelve Fund was a great deal bigger. It would nearly all go on paint. Now that Size Twelve had his collar and was fed for nothing, and while he stayed healthy, there was nothing else to spend the money on.

But the strangest thing came at the end of the evening when the parents were served weak tea and rather damp biscuits. Taffy walked among them, holding Size Twelve, and every parent crowded around to greet and stroke him. Almost, Mrs Forbes thought, as if he were the Prince of Wales on a visit, or even a strange small furry god, whom to touch was good luck.

Everybody in the school was thrilled, except Edward Druel, who was the worst boy of all. *Much* worse than Taffy Thomas. Taffy told everybody what he wanted, and if he got it, he left people in peace. You knew where you were with Taffy. He was a tribal leader and if you kept his laws you were safe.

Edward Druel was evil for the sake of it. He pulled wings off butterflies, and laughed as he watched them crawling about helpless. He tortured people by putting their heads down the toilet and pulling the chain, just for

31

the hell of it. He even did it to some girls, in the boys' toilet. You never knew where you were with Edward Druel; never felt safe. And all his followers were the same. He and Taffy had halved the school between them. Taffy was king of 4A and Druel was the king of 4B.

Now things had changed. Taffy Thomas was famous, had his picture in the paper. Taffy Thomas's father was boss of the parents' committee. Taffy Thomas had turned respectable and had private chats with the Head. And Taffy Thomas got more and more people in his gang, while Edward Druel's gang dwindled.

Edward Druel knew very well whose fault it was. That damned cat.

He knew what he would do. He would catch that cat and kill it. Slowly.

Meanwhile, Taffy and Size Twelve and the whole school prospered. Several more local freebies sent photographers, getting into the act. Even the local newspaper that people had to pay for came along.

And then one morning, before school, Taffy knocked on Mrs Forbes' door, and came in and threw a large wad of fivers on to her desk.

'F'the fund,' he muttered. Mrs Forbes stared at him aghast. What had he done? Robbed a bank?

'Where . . . did you get . . . that?' She wondered wildly whether the Size Twelve Fund could afford a lawyer for Taffy.

'The big newspapers came. The *Mail* and *Mirror* and *Sun*. We wouldn't show them Size Twelve 'til they coughed up. Then they coughed up a bit more when I got Miss Morgan to hold Size Twelve an' cross her legs. She's got smashing legs – best in the school. They liked that. Specially when she hitched up her skirt a bit . . .'

'Taffy . . . how much?'

'Five hundred quid. That's nothing. You know how much they'll pay for that kind of thing . . .?' Taffy's voice rose to an indignant squeak. 'I reckon we was robbed. If the *News of the World* turns up, or the *Express*, it won't half cost them . . .'

The bell went, and he left. Mrs Forbes could hardly count the money for wondering what County Hall would say.

chapter 6

Edward Druel laid his plans well, he thought. He had spent a lot of time spying on Size Twelve, from a safe distance. He had noticed that at four o'clock, Size Twelve went off the school premises through a gap in the fence by the old bike-shed. And there were some nice strong beams holding up the bike-shed roof . . .

One afternoon, after school, Edward Druel lurked in the bike shed, with a tin of best red salmon, a tin-opener and a long length of rope. He opened the salmon, and spread it over the bike-shed floor. Then he called to Size Twelve as he passed. Size Twelve, nose working at the delicious smell,

36

trotted over all trusting, and began to lick up the salmon. Edward Druel pretended to stroke him as he ate, and carefully slid the rope through his collar and tied a knot . . . Then all he
had to do was pull on the rope, and there was Size Twelve swinging and kicking like a condemned murderer, being choked to death by his fine new collar. A great sport!

Except . . . perhaps . . . Size Twelve knew a bit more about things than Edward Druel thought.

There was a piece of stretchy elastic set in Size Twelve's collar, for just such an occasion. Now, under the kicking choking weight of the cat's body, the elastic began to stretch and the collar pass over Size Twelve's head.

And at the same moment, Taffy Thomas, who'd been having his usual word with the Head, to make sure the school was running OK, came to collect his old bike, and saw Size Twelve swinging and Edward Druel laughing.

Now Taffy Thomas and Edward Druel had never fought each other, though they were both terrible fighters. They knew they were evenly matched, and that if they fought, the winner would get hurt as badly as the loser. So they'd kept out of each other's way till now.

But when Taffy saw the great love of his life swinging, and Edward Druel laughing, all sense left him. He went for Edward Druel like Genghis Khan at the Great Wall of China.

The noise of the punching and screeching and swearing and kicking reached Mrs Forbes as she walked to her car. She had the impression that the old bike shed was jumping up and down on its own, and about to collapse. She ran like she hadn't run in years.

Too late. She found Taffy Thomas with

one eye closing, a bitten wrist and blood streaming from his nose like a red Niagara, all down his 'Stop the bloody whaling' T-shirt. Edward Druel was just a moaning heap lying in the corner.

'What have you *done*, Taffy?' she cried, trying to make her voice sound as shocked as possible, though part of her recognised Druel's leather jacket and thought secretly, 'About time, too!'

'He tried to hang the cat, Miss,' said Taffy triumphantly through snorts of bubbly blood. 'He tried to hang Size Twelve!' And he pointed to where the rope and empty collar were still swinging, though Size Twelve was sitting on the ground under it, making some attempt to wash himself, but watching all three of them and purring loudly.

'I shall have to ring for an ambulance,' said Mrs Forbes faintly.

'Why not the refuse-cart, miss?' Taffy

Thomas wiped his nose with the back of his hand and surveyed the result with scientific interest.

Just then, Edward Druel got up slowly, and walked away like a kangaroo with two broken legs; without saying a word, though if looks could kill, Taffy and Mrs Forbes and Size Twelve would all have been dead.

'He'll live,' said Taffy. 'Pity!'

'I . . . I . . . shall have to suspend him,' said Mrs Forbes despairingly. 'Trying to hang the school cat!' She was despairing because she'd tried suspending Edward Druel before. But the gentlemen at County Hall said that Edward Druel was only 'educationally deprived' and in need of care and understanding, and insisted that he be returned to school immediately . . .

'Don't bother, miss,' said Taffy Thomas. 'When all the kids find out what he's done . . .'

'I'll have no more violence!' cried Mrs Forbes hysterically, for she was having visions of Edward Druel hanging by the neck from the school lamp-post, which hadn't worked for thirty years.

'We won't lay a finger on him, Miss,' said Taffy Thomas. 'Promise!'

And with that, she had to be content.

Taffy was as good as his word. He made Edward Druel's remaining followers an offer they couldn't possibly refuse. They accepted swiftly, and became Taffy's henchmen.

As for the rest of the children, nobody at all spoke to Edward Druel, ever again. When he walked round the playground a gap opened up around him, a gap ten yards wide. The kids who ran the tuck-shop turned deaf when he asked for a Mars Bar. If he took his eyes off his schoolbag for a moment, it vanished. When he came to school on his bike, it was found tied to the top of the school lamp-post. With *chains*. In class, no-one would sit near him; everyone complained of a funny smell . . . as if a cat had peed on him. Size Twelve was shooed away; as if Size Twelve needed telling.

After four days, Edward Druel refused to come to school any more. County Hall declared him 'a school-refuser.' People only heard dark rumours of him after that. People said he'd been sent to the child psychiatrists, which was worse than being thrown to the wolves.

Chapter 7

Everyone at the school became very happy. Even Mrs Forbes – though she walked round the school with her shoulders hunched, as if expecting a thunderbolt from County Hall.

That was even before they heard that the telly was coming, to film Size Twelve. That caused an uproar. Mr Thomas, about thirty dads and some mums, too, arrived with paint-brushes, and worked on the school until midnight for a week. Mrs Forbes not only spent all the Size Twelve Fund on paint, she also spent what was left of the General Purpose Fund, the meagre profits of the tuck shop, and fifty pounds of her own money.

Then everyone turned up, and dusted and

polished and cleaned the windows you could hardly see out of, and put up posters, mainly of cats, that they'd bought at W. H. Smith's.

Then the thunderbolt fell. County Hall sent an Inspector to say that the telly people couldn't come; they were not to be allowed to film. Against county policy . . .

In vain, Mrs Forbes argued. The inspector was truly amazed that the school looked so spick and span. He was truly amazed at how happy all the children were, and how well-behaved. But county policy was county policy. He kept on saying this rather desperately, even when Mr Thomas and the other dads turned up for an evening's painting, and looked like they were going to stay around for an evening's lynching . . .

Mrs Forbes fell silent at last, staring bleakly at the crumbling of her dream . . . so much hope . . . parents and children . . . brought to ruin by County Hall.

And then, in her desperation, she thought up her Great Lie. The first lie she had told in thirty years, really.

'But I've spoken to the MPs . . .'

A thin film of sweat broke out on the Inspector's face. The town had two MPs, one Tory and one Labour. They couldn't stand each other, they didn't agree about anything. Except one thing. They both loved getting on the telly. More than anything. Even sharing with a cat . . .

The Inspector fled to consult his bosses, who like all councils were terrified of MPs. His car shot out of the school yard like the starting-grid of a Grand Prix.

Mrs Forbes, striving to square her conscience, fled indoors to the phone and asked for the number of the Palace of Westminster.

It became a truly great day for everybody.

Flags and bunting.

Exhibitions of work.

Displays of country dancing.

Both MPs.

And not just ITV but BBC regional as well.

The Tory MP cuddled the cat for the cameras and called what the school had done a splendid example of private sector initiative. He said he had offers for the school from friends in industry. Second-hand computers. Maybe a second-hand minibus . . .

The Labour MP cuddled the cat for the cameras and called what the school had done an example of community action by hard-pressed working people who really cared about their children's future. He promised to harry the County Council until the parents and children of Valley Road got all the things they were really entitled to. He

47

would, too. He was as much feared at
County Hall as Taffy Thomas was at Valley
Road Primary.

Size Twelve was very gracious, and didn't scratch anybody.

Taffy Thomas wore a suit specially bought for the occasion and looked more like the oriental god of good fortune than ever.

And then, at the end, Size Twelve vanished as he usually did.

But this time, it was for good.

Chapter 8

Taffy Thomas sat on his bed in his pyjamas, as still as a stone.

'I can't do a thing with him,' said Taffy's mum. 'Three days, and he won't eat, or anything.'

'Leave him to me,' said Swotty Knowles. Taffy's mum did; there was nothing else she could think of to do. She was at the end of her tether.

Swotty sat down beside the stillness of Taffy.

'Weren't Edward Druel that got him,' he said. 'He's at a school for the maladjusted in the Outer Hebrides.'

'I know *that*,' said Taffy, and relapsed

back into his stony stillness.

'The kids have searched everywhere. Allotments, the lot. They had to break into some of the garages. They even asked the *police*. Nobody's seen him. We even dragged the canal . . .'

'Yeah,' said Taffy, hardly bothering to move his lips.

'He can't just have vanished into thin air . . . unless . . .'

'Unless *what*?' The terrible pain and rage inside Taffy came out in a sudden spit, like a striking snake. Swotty felt that Taffy might lash out at any moment. But Swotty went on sitting there, like the faithful soul he was.

'Unless he was a . . . *god*.'

'Don't talk wet. Cats can't be gods.'

'Cats was gods in Ancient Egypt. I looked it up in books. All the people worshipped them, and if anyone tried to harm a cat they were beaten to death.'

'Pity Druel hadn't lived in Ancient Egypt,' said Taffy, with a first sign of returning life.

'People worshipped them, and they prophesied the future by waggling their ears.'

'Who, the people?'

'No, the cats, stupid.' It was a sign of the decline of Taffy that Swotty dared to call him stupid. But Taffy never stirred.

'The cats in Ancient Egypt made everything right for everybody. Ancient Egypt was the happiest place in history.

Nobody got massacred or anything. I think Size Twelve was a sort of god, sent to make our school better. And now his work is done, he's gone on to higher things.'

Taffy remembered that parents' evening in the school hall. The night everyone had wanted to stroke the cat, how they'd crowded round to touch him, as if he was the Prince of Wales or . . . a god. He smiled faintly at the memory.

'Mebbe he *has* gone on to higher things . . .'

'Like some posh grammar school or big comprehensive that's in a mess . . .' said Swotty coaxingly.

'But they're all in a mess,' said Taffy. 'We can't search every school in the city.'

'We could try!'

'No,' said Taffy. 'This time he'll have gone for something really big!'

'Like Lunn Road Tech?'

Taffy looked on him with scorn. '*Really* big,' he repeated. There was a rasp of impatience in his voice that told Swotty that life was returning. 'Like the university.'

Swotty goggled. When Taffy said 'big' he really meant it.

Chapter 9

They went down to the university disguised as students. Taffy wanted to put on his best suit, that he'd worn on the telly. But Swotty said students just wore worn-out jeans and sloppy sweaters and anoraks covered with badges. And long scarves.

So they went down looking very much like themselves, except for the long scarves they'd borrowed from their mum and sister. Swotty knew where the university was. He hoped to go there himself one day, and his hopes had grown brighter since Size Twelve came.

They got off the bus and walked up to the Porter's lodge.

And, unbelievably and miraculously, there was a black cat sitting on the window sill of the porter's lodge.

'S'im,' said Swotty.

'What's happened to his collar?' demanded Taffy, in a carrying voice.

The porter put his head out of the window and said, 'You kids, get lost, quick!'

'I intend to come here to study,' said Swotty in his poshest voice. 'Eventually.'

'Ho, really?' said the porter, not at all impressed. 'I shall hawait that hevent with great interest.' He was a very large man with a peaked cap and big black moustache. He looked like he might get nasty if he was handled wrong.

'How long you had your cat, mister?' asked Taffy, hurriedly, in a very respectful voice.

'Turned up about three days ago,' said the porter. 'A hamiable beast. I think we shall hadopt it.'

Taffy looked hard at the cat. Was it Size Twelve? It had big enough feet; and notches in its ears from fighting. Its expression was friendly, but guarded. As if . . . it was a spy meeting an old friend while on a secret mission, and not wanting to be recognised.

But Taffy hadn't met any other black cats in his short life. It was impossible to be *sure*.

'Why did you take its collar off?' Taffy asked suddenly.

The porter looked terribly guilty for a moment, then shouted, 'Go on, get lost, or

I'll take my foot to your backsides.'

There was no arguing with him in that mood. They both knew he meant it. But Swotty drew himself up to his full height and said, 'When you see your vice-chancellor, give him a message from me. Tell him that things are going to get a lot better round here, soon.'

That did it. The porter erupted out of his lodge. They had to take to their heels.

But when they looked back from a safe distance, the black cat, still sitting on the window sill, seemed to give them a conspiratorial grin. And with that they had to be content.

They sat on the bus home, telling each other that it *had* been Size Twelve, over and over again. Until finally Swotty said doubtfully, 'Well even if it is him, we won't have him any more.'

They both sighed. The weight of the school without Size Twelve hung above them like a leaden sky.

'But even if it's *not* him,' said Swotty, 'he might come strolling back some day. To see how we're getting on without him. We don't want to go back to . . . he'd be disappointed. He'd feel we'd let him down.'

'He can't be *everywhere* at once,' said Taffy in a low voice. 'There's too many places in the world . . .'

'We'd better go on running things the way he'd have wanted them . . .'

Taffy squared his shoulders, and something of the old look came back in his face.

'We can *try*,' he said.